The Novel
and Other
Incidents

Charlotte Harker

TSL Publications

First published in Great Britain in 2022
By TSL Publications, Rickmansworth

Copyright © 2022 Charlotte Harker

ISBN / 978-1-914245-92-3

Cover and Illustrations by Charlotte Harker

Contents

4

A Continuing Professional Development Obsessed English Health and Safety Official Visits the Valencian Town of Bunol in Spain for the Annual August La Tomatina Festival

He gathered up his clipboard and looked at the categories; accessibility, cleanliness, provision of public conveniences, opening hours, participant numbers, police presence, security measures and noise levels. He seemed to have brought a characteristic thoroughness to the template.

He looked in the mirror. His hair was neatly combed over and his glasses were clean and gleaming. His freshly washed and ironed khaki shorts and shirt were smart and his new sandals with Velcro fastenings were both practical and fashionable. 'Super' he said to himself.

He stepped outside of the very reasonably priced guest house onto the cobbled street. Before he had a chance to score a zero rating in the participant numbers column and adding a note that noise levels were exceeding safe limits, a large tomato hit him squarely on the ear. The clear juices, ruptured red skin and seeds which had not lodged in his ear canal slowly dripped down the side of his head and neck.

This contact was soon followed by two more of the red fruit or vegetables which hit him on the glasses at high velocity. These were thrown by a tall black haired woman who screamed in delight at her accuracy.

It was only a few minutes before his khaki outfit was mostly stained red. His clipboard had gone. He was just in time to see it being thrown in a bin. In the next moment the black haired woman had wound her way through the crowd toward him and grabbed his hand and led him into the fray. Tomatoes were being hurled in all directions.

No one ever found out what happened to him. He never returned to work on the following Monday. Despite efforts to locate and make contact the only information as to his where-abouts amounted to a rumour of an unknown English speaking bearded man living with goats in the Pyrenees.

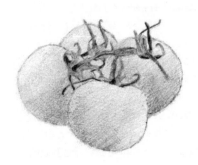

How To Make Yourself Scarce

1. Politely inform your acquaintance that you have another appointment at an unspecified time in an unspecified place. Resist giving in to the pressure of requests for more details and sceptical looks from your companion and then excuse yourself.

Practise being inscrutable.

2. Sit at the back of the auditorium near a door. If the performance is too embarrassing, noisy or impenetrable leave quietly under the cover of darkness at a moment when everyone else is fully engaged with the art.

Practise identifying and acting upon the right moment.

3. Divert attention away from oneself by looking into the middle distance and feigning surprise at spotting something unusual going on. Slip away as the focus moves to the phantom occurrence.

Practise in the mirror making a convincing expression of surprise.

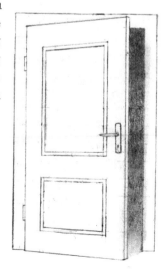

Storm Flower

The lightest of rain showers seemed to bludgeon the flower. When the rain and the wind went wilder I was concerned and I watched as the thin white petals hung on. Water slid off as if the flower sobbed under the weight of the onslaught. The odds of survival seemed slim as raindrops hit the flower at a quicker and quicker velocity and the wind howled louder bending the stems to a near horizontal.

On the following day when the storm had passed I was afraid I would discover the flower had been crushed under the weight of the heavy rain and partly buried in a shallow grave. I thought I would find some scattered petals and broken stems where the wind had torn the flower apart limb by limb.

But the flower was there and displayed a renewed vibrancy as it demonstrated that strength was found through vulnerability.

The Snow Globe of Mallorca

I wish I had attended the marketing meeting at the traders' cartel at the tourism office in downtown Las Palmas when their latest gift, a snow globe from Mallorca was unveiled on that Wednesday afternoon when temperatures had reached an exhausting 30 degrees Celsius.

I imagined the little transparent clear dome and white flakes settled on the model of the church and the town square.

I visualised the moment when one of the traders picked up the dome and shook it. I observed the concentration of all of them as the flakes moved storm like in that miniature weather system and then settled on the cobbles and formed deep drifts up the sides of the Catholic Church completely burying a donkey and a group of figures standing near the entrance.

It was clear that the traders wanted to imagine what the white flakes would be like falling as heavy snow and settling on their town.

In my imaginings I detected a desire for respite from the unrelenting heat and a collective concern about the effect of rising yearly temperatures.

Of course they could have gone to the mainland to experience it but they all agreed that having your own snow, however modest, was better than using somebody else's.

Archie

'I wonder what Archie thinks? I will ask him.'
I did but he didn't seem to have a detailed
opinion. He said that I should not take it so
personally. He said that that person was having
a bad day so his invective was not my fault. He
said that I was not to blame. Archie thought
that it was the result of a cocktail of
misunderstandings, miscommunication and
misplaced assumptions.

I did agree but I could not help but feel
victimised. Archie said that narcissism was
unhealthy. I recognised that, but surely all
this self obsession is self preservation. How
much do I care for anyone except myself. How
much would I sacrifice for someone else? Well
that is an exploratory question, though I
cannot allow myself to think I would put anyone
else's wellbeing before my own.

I noticed that Archie was staring at me. He
seemed concerned. I realised that I had said
all that out loud.

Archie said I should take up a hobby. I agreed
that was a good idea but asked him what he would
suggest. I then remembered that I don't like
hobbies and told him so before he could make
any suggestions. I said that hobbies seemed so
insufficient as if you are not taking an
endeavour seriously enough. I thought that if
you are going to do something then you need to
do it to get noticed. I do want to be noticed

don't I? There I was again: narcissism, self obsession, attention-seeking; wringing all the joy from hobbies.

It was clear Archie was now exasperated and said rather sternly that I should take a long hard look at myself in the mirror but as he was saying this he realised the error in his suggestion.

Unfortunately I was buoyed by this encouragement and I rushed off to sit in a room to deconstruct my future for the rest of the day, but then who knew how long that would really take.

Blue Cutlery

I don't like my blue cutlery. I call it blue cutlery because of the colour of the handles which have a frosted glass appearance. I don't know why I bought them. Was it because they had the unusual handle?

The photograph on the label of the box was of a Manhattan loft apartment with a close-up of an oak table showing cutlery arranged on it. I imagined myself living in this apartment. I had bought the cutlery, hadn't I? I was fielding calls from Berlin, Paris and Shanghai. I had just finished a meal of nouvelle cuisine.

But I don't live in Manhattan, do I?

I live in a flat in suburban London and as far as I can remember I have never taken a call from Berlin, Paris or Shanghai. The closest I came to that experience was when I received a text from a distressed friend in Dover. She had got on the wrong bus at Victoria Station. She had meant to go to Brighton.

I do have an oak table though, which I bought at a discount from someone calling himself Dave from Hounslow. The table was discounted because it had a crack in it.

There didn't seem to be any cracks in the oak table in the photograph on the cutlery box and now my blue cutlery is falling to pieces. It is not very well made. It doesn't seem so stylish anymore. I don't think it ever truly was. Why didn't I just buy steel cutlery without a fancy handle?

The Crossing

I was walking down the street the other day and I noticed a large number of smartly dressed people on the opposite side of the road at a zebra crossing. I went over to investigate.

An exchange of routine pleasantries and carefully phrased questions revealed they were lawyers holding their annual conference. After many years of feeling unfairly maligned in some quarters not helped by major literary interventions such as 'the first thing we do, let's kill all the lawyers' from Henry VI by William Shakespeare, they had decided to take to the streets to be more in touch with, in their words, 'the people'.

They were feeling hurt by the suggestion that their profession across the centuries had fallen victim to accusations of questionable moral and ethical standards.

A zebra crossing seemed appropriate since apparently as a pedestrian if you are knocked down whilst crossing a zebra crossing it is possible to make a claim against the driver. This made the lawyers feel good as from their point of view, in this situation, they were most definitely fighting on behalf of the underdog or as they liked to say 'our valued clients'.

Of course, the zebra was none too pleased by this conference at its crossing and had been squashed against the crash barrier railings on the roadside, such was the number of lawyers who had congregated. The zebra was very cross indeed. In fact the zebras were annoyed by lawyers always wanting to meet at their crossings and felt they were being taken for granted.

To add insult to injury if a zebra was knocked down at a crossing the zebra would be unable to make a claim since firstly, it was a zebra and did not have the capacity to fill in the forms and secondly, lawyers do not act on behalf of zebras. They were keen to emphasise this in order to dispel yet another misconception that if the fee was right they would represent anyone or anything with a pulse.

Bouquet

As he placed the bouquet of flowers on the table, he said that they were not for me. I felt a new wound which was sharp and keen. Old cuts opened too which I recognised for what they were and with a sense of familiarity. Of course, I carried on because I had to. I continued as a ship might in a storm making slow progress but progress nonetheless and correcting its course as it edged its way up and down high slopes of moving water. I had tried my best to avoid disturbance but sometimes there was no way round it and so the turmoil had to be faced head on. He had said it all with those flowers. Eventually I accepted that they were there and I generally ignored them as I cut through my day, although I caught myself admiring their beauty which was at times irresistible.

The following day they had gone and all that remained on the table was a single petal that had cut loose from the rest of the flowers.

Man Killed by a Collection of Charles Dickens Novels in Antique Hardback

A section of the library was cordoned off. A crowd of people looked on in silence behind the newly erected barrier. A body was lying in a pool of blood under a pile of books at the foot of collapsed shelving in the English Literature section of the library.

The paramedics had never come across such injuries. *A Tale of Two Cities* had inflicted deep lacerations in the poor librarian's arm, the gold metal edge of the book cutting deep. A copy of *Little Dorrit* had broken open his skull. The impact of a metal clasp had caused an indent in his forehead, and *Great Expectations* had smashed a kneecap. One of the paramedics said he had never seen paper cuts like it. They had been caused by the gold leaf edging of *A Christmas Carol*.

As I reflected on this scene I wanted to find an underlying message or profound metaphorical observation. Reaching for Richelieu's line 'the pen is mightier than the sword' seemed weak and disrespectful to the unfortunate librarian.

As I found out, the cause of this incident originated from a breakdown in communication between the designers of the newly installed shelving and the size and weight requirements of this particular singular library's stock of books.

As a result the shelving had collapsed, someone had died and a war of words broke out between a collection of interior designers and an army of devoted bookworms.

This explanation seemed far more tragic than any erudite quotation could ever express.

25 Canary Villas

25 Canary Villas was the scene of a fracas last Tuesday evening at a meeting of the Role Playing Board Gamers Association. Police were called and arrests were made for public order offences.

At 10.15 p.m. neighbours reported hearing shouting and the sound of smashing glass. Eyewitnesses said they saw Bob the Builder and Danger Mouse fighting in the front garden.

The Police issued a statement in which they said the trouble started when Thelma from *Scooby-Doo* was accused of money laundering during a game of Monopoly. This dispute escalated into verbal abuse exchanged across gaming tables. The confrontations eventually spilled onto the street.

The organisers, Darth Vader and The Clangers, apologised to neighbours for the disruption and upsetting scenes adding they had made every effort to organise the evening to keep flashpoints to a minimum. Those arrested will appear in court later this month.

In a further statement Police appealed for witnesses and information connected with the disappearance of Dennis the Menace and Gnasher from the scene. They are wanted in connection with alleged criminal damage.

Let Go or be Dragged

Last night an 18th century man upturned my bookshelves and rearranged the furniture. This was another visit from a poltergeist who claimed to have dated and then been dumped by Jane Austen, according to his quill pen scribblings in the inside covers of my copies of *Sanditon* and *Sense and Sensibility.* He revealed she had told him one day that 'he had delighted her enough.'

He suspected her decision had more to do with the inescapable fact that he was not in possession of a large wad of cash or recipient of a trust fund. Though he conceded that since she had rejected him he was suffering from paranoia and couldn't truly believe that Jane could be quite that shallow.

This troubled ghoul had been hassling me for some time. Now tired and perplexed once again I began the task of clearing up. I reassembled the settee and brought the kitchen chairs in from the street and looked for the dog, which had disappeared.

I was informed by a neighbour, who had received a text message from a friend at an airport, of a sighting in a departure lounge. A Springer Spaniel with a cabin bag was seen waiting in a line to board a jet to an island in the Mediterranean.

I collected my thoughts, and considered my options. I decided I needed to reach an arrangement with this ruffled Georgian relic, clearly lacking in self-esteem and enduring the pain of unrequited love, for far too long in my opinion.

I recalled in Zen it is said, 'Let Go or be Dragged'. This brought me a modicum of calm. I wrote this wisdom down on a sheet of paper, and placed it on a table, in the hope that it would also help my supernatural intruder.

I then shouted out: 'Listen ghost, continue if you must but leave the drinks cabinet as you found it and please keep the noise down!' I read out some other house rules, packed my bag and left my home, still in monstrous chaos, as I embarked on a search for my, evidently sensible, Spaniel.

The Kitchen Clock

The kitchen clock was ticking very loudly this morning. At least I thought each strike was louder than usual. Perhaps my sense of the passage of time had become more acute, but I was sure the clock was trying to tell me something.
This is what it said:

Okay, here is another and another and another. I could do this in my sleep. I do this while everyone else is sleeping. I don't get any thanks. I have been doing this for as long as I can remember. I need a change. Even the switch to British Summer time was not enough to raise my mood. That was just a temporary respite. I am so bored. So bored.

I haven't even got an alarm, what with me being a kitchen wall clock. But then I am too old for alarms. They are for other timepieces which like the adrenalin rush of a repetitive buzz, a bell on a high speed setting or an extract of Cyndi Lauper's rendition of 'Time After Time'.

I am so bored.

My battery is adequate, although I do feel a bit of a twinge, a sense of slowing down. Well that is something to look forward to. A change of battery. I always get a frisson when there is an initial surge as it kicks into life. It is temporary though. Isn't that the point? It is all temporary so I might as well make the best of it and enjoy the view from up here.

Wow, I have seen everything in this kitchen. Rows, laughter, tears and sex. Parties, silence and intense discussions. It all comes and then it goes. I pass. I pass. I pass the time by passing the time.

I have such an influence on people's moods.

Ooh, I haven't got the time! Ooh, I'm late! Ooh, we've got plenty of time.

Well you haven't, have you? My insisting rhythm is trying to point this out. You don't. Everything is finite and all things will pass.

I'm so bored.

A Horse Walks into a Bar[1]

A horse walks into a bar. The barman did not say 'Why the long face?'

Before the barman could proceed the horse explained: 'I am a horse. I have a long face. I am a grazing animal and evolved in open grassland. With a small stomach and a diet high in rough forage, I spend a large amount of time eating with my head down at ground level. Having a long face places my range of vision, in this position, at a level which allows for greater awareness of my surroundings. This is important because I am a prey animal and my primary defence is running away. That's evolution for you. Happy now?'

The horse ordered drinks. 'Bacardi and Coke with ice and a straw. An orange juice for my rider.'

The barman served the drinks and turned to the horse for payment, since the horse seemed to be doing all the talking.

The horse said, 'My rider is paying you idiot. I am a horse. I don't have any money.'

The rider paid the barman. They finished their drinks quickly and the horse turned to leave banging its head on a low beam. The horse was drunk and not concentrating. The rider ducked beneath the beam as they made for the exit.

---

[1] 'A Horse Walks into a Bar' was placed first in the October 2019 *Blue Animal* literary magazine monthly flash fiction competition.

Outside they passed a queue of assorted fauna. A swan, followed by a cat, a bear, a squirrel, an otter and so on down the line. Each was clutching typed scripts in whatever means of clutching, evolution had deemed appropriate, beak, paw, and pouch, for example.

A sign read –

Today. Auditions for new replacements or variations on 'A Horse Walks into a Bar'

'I thought that went quite well,' said the horse. The rider nodded in agreement.

Flight of Fancy

In 2015, 'New Horizons', an interplanetary space craft, which was launched in 2006, flew by the dwarf planet Pluto and its moons. This spacecraft was the fifth artificial object to achieve the escape velocity needed to leave the solar system. Near earth the approximate speed of 'New Horizons' was 37,000 miles per hour. Later in its journey it slowed to a relatively more pedestrian 29,000 miles per hour.

This spacecraft is comparable in size to a grand piano and in its shape has been compared to a piano glued to a cocktail bar sized satellite dish.

I could not let this information pass by unnoticed and so I paused to reflect on and write about it. Naturally, the image of a grand piano, a Steinway perhaps, travelling through space at a mind bending speed came into view.

At this piano was seated a be-suited pianist, playing, in between sipping on a cocktail called the Asteroid Belter, as he travelled through space at eight miles per second.

Writing this I was seated on a chair at a desk in a room. On this desk was a cup of tea. Despite appearances none of these items including myself is stationary as we are all on a planet which is rotating on its axis at about 1,000 miles per hour whilst orbiting the Sun at an average speed of 67,000 miles per hour. Even the tea doesn't spill.

Oh!! Everything is moving. I imagined myself stepping off for a moment to observe this spectacle and to have a rest and I wondered how the pianist was getting on.

He never writes.

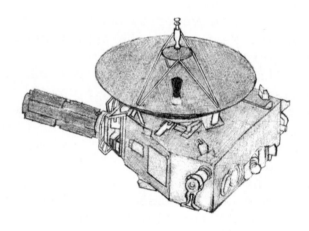

Celia the Squirrel Wins Booker Prize

In a shock announcement and unprecedented in literary competition history the Booker Prize has been awarded to a late entry.

The coveted prize has been given to *Nuts in Autumn* by Celia the Squirrel. It is Celia's debut novel and has been described as a masterpiece of modern literature. Translated from the original squirrel, *Nuts in Autumn* spans several decades and generations of a family of middle-class Squirrels and draws upon Celia's own experience growing up in suburban Middlesex, as well as archive material of her ancestors, originally from Buckinghamshire. The novel explores love, loss and conflict and of course the complex skill of collecting and storing nuts.

Senior editor, Geoff the Fox, from Literary Magazine, *Words from the Woods*, praised Celia's winning novel by saying that it was a masterclass in how to write a family saga.

So that's all very exciting, isn't it?

The Last Letter Writer

In a room of a semi-detached house in a town in the Midlands there is a writer who is the last person in the country to write letters in ink on paper. The last letter writer.

A crowd is gathered around a window of her home, watching as she sits at her desk writing her latest correspondence. This crowd is the most recent official tour arranged to mark a special occasion. Many people on the tour don't know how to hold a fountain pen in their hand and so they witness an exotic act as the last letter writer's hand guides the nib across the page, crafting words and sentences in looping handwriting slanted to the right.

They watch as her thoughts are applied to the page. She is writing a letter to herself as she is the last letter writer in a closed loop of correspondence. She never tires of the joy in receiving a hand-delivered written communication and in reading her letters which reveal herself again and again.

A former postman volunteered to come out of retirement to fulfil the task of delivering her correspondence as he regarded it to be a valuable community service. Once again he makes his way through the crowd who look on in fascination as he slides another letter through the letterbox. The last letter writer makes her way to the hallway and the door to pick up the letter from the floor. It is her 100th birthday but this is not a birthday card from the King.

The crowd wait to see if she switches on her computer and accesses her emails to see that special birthday message. She has not switched her computer on for many years and so will need to be prompted to see this particular form of communicating birthday greetings. She is the last letter writer and it is unlikely she will care for such a gesture.

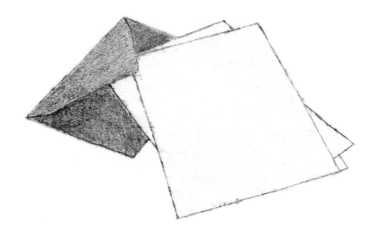

Alone

I am so anti-social I don't even have
imaginary friends.

Step Outside If You Think You're Hard Enough

'Come on then, if you think you're hard enough'. So I do, I step outside and cross a threshold; I cross the line; I walk the line; I take in a deep breath and inhale an air thick with fear and loathing, with judgement and impatience, with self-interest and aggression. I fight my way through and when I return home, some the wiser, I am exhausted.

I only went out to post a letter.

Takk

'Takk,'
I said clearly and enthusiastically, as the bus driver handed me the ticket.

'Takk' means thank you in Norwegian. I had learnt this from a phrase book along with other words and phrases in preparation for my stay in Bergen. I thought it would be a pleasant surprise for the recipient who would undoubtedly appreciate the effort I had clearly made to at least learn something of the native tongue. I had always thought that one's experience as a traveller in another country is so much richer if one can see an appreciative response to such effort.

Unfortunately, my excited anticipation of a positive interaction after I had said my Norwegian 'thank you' was greeted with the descending of an icy atmosphere. The bus driver looked at me with a mixture of hostility, amusement and concern and I am sure I heard a barely suppressed laugh in the gradually forming queue behind me.

In the manner of the quiet clearing of a low lying fog over a fjord I realised that I was not in Norway, I was boarding a bus in Upminster.

I really must stop day dreaming.

About Edward[1]

Many years ago at a funeral I overheard one of the mourners say, to no one in particular, 'If I knew then what I know now, my life would have been different. It would have turned out for the better. We would have been together. We would have been happy.'

I was both moved and unsettled by the outburst of this disappointed and rueful man. The mood of his regret was visceral and the thought of my own mortality inevitable. Since then I have been taking stock; revisiting my past, as if I were watching a film of it, stopping at particular moments and replaying the scenes.

Now, as I recall the disappointment of the old man at the funeral, I gaze through the sitting room window, to the other side of the street and I think of my friend, Edward. I have not seen him for many years. I picture him as a teenager. It is the most persistent memory I have.

We had been friends since we were twelve years old. Together we imagined ourselves as a force for the defence of whatever was good and kind. We liked the same music, as long as our parents didn't like it, and the same books and films. We shared a love of the subversive, the absurd, the deadpan and the artful. We were high on our youth. Our friendship was intense and was always evolving.

---

[1] 'About Edward' was shortlisted for the LB Tower Hamlets Writeidea Literary Festival Short Story Prize 2019

We would meet often. At home we would sit and talk out of earshot of my parents, or 'the 1950s' as we affectionately called them. Edward was witty. He always made me laugh. I indulged him and did not realise how his influence brought out a dry and whimsical side of my personality too. This was good for me because I was painfully shy back then. With Edward it was always so much easier and I was happy and comfortable when I was with him.

Sometimes we would cycle along the country lanes between the fields, close to where we lived and often went to a favourite bridge over a river, which wound its way through the flat landscape. I smile at the thought of having a favourite bridge. But it was our place. Close to it stood an isolated church, which had no roof. I always thought that curious. It stood in the grounds of a small churchyard, the perimeter of which you could walk in minutes. We both adored this church. At least I thought Edward did. I am sure he did, though he often seemed underwhelmed. Now I know this was deceptive. He was much more thoughtful and reflective.

As we arrived at the bridge, we would see the church directly ahead as we leaned our bikes against the railings. We would always take a moment to look at the church which stood in the setting of a group of trees.

One day we stepped over a stile and made our way down a steep bank to the riverside. This place was so quiet. The river flowed swiftly and flashes of light reflected off the surface of the water.

We lay together on the bank. I was reading and Edward was asleep. We had been there for hours and did not notice the fall of dusk. Edward suddenly sat bolt upright. He seemed anxious and agitated. I didn't say anything. As our eyes were adjusting, we turned to look at the bridge. We were sure a figure was standing next to our bikes and looking in our direction.

As the light faded the shape of the figure seemed to shift but never disappear. We both stood up and slowly made our way to the bridge. There was no one there. We should have known better how the fading light could tempt us with illusions.

As we cycled home, the summer air on our faces was fresh and invigorating. I could see Edward was relieved but still shaken by the apparition. He was so sensitive.

We said goodnight on the corner of a road which lead towards our respective homes in opposite directions. At these moments Edward always became serious as if he wanted to stay there and talk more. He always seemed frustrated and disappointed when we parted.

Years later I realised that I was an important part of his teenage life. When we were not together I think he thought of me often. He deserved more respect than I gave him. I did not appreciate how much he adored me. I don't even think he realised the growing strength and resilience of his affection.

On some occasions he would say that he did not want to see me any more as a friend. This always upset me and our conversation would slide into pointless argument. I did not understand. But I was not able to imagine him as my boyfriend.

It took me years to understand he loved me and that I felt the same. On one particularly notable occasion he telephoned me and told me so quite unexpectedly. He meant it and I knew it. By that time it was too late, I was married and Edward had moved away.

The years passed by. We spoke on the phone and we met when my husband was away on business. When we did contact each other we effortlessly picked up where we had left off. We behaved like teenagers again. Edward would make me laugh and I indulged his endless flights of fancy, which he delighted in sharing with me.

He was often on his own. He never wanted to talk openly about the fact that he had been alone for a long time. He denied this bothered him. I did not believe his indifference and I also knew it hurt him when he spoke to me.

I have never been clear as to what kind of love I have for Edward, but it was more than the love of a friend and it has endured. It was never straightforward where he was concerned. He was so different to the other men I had dated and the one I married.

My contact with Edward gradually reduced to almost nothing, to the barest thread of a connection on social media. I feel sorry I have lost touch with him. Now I am upset when I imagine him alone and disappointed. I desperately want to believe that is not so. I recall one particular time when we were together and how, I recognise now, our lives turned on that time.

We were both at colleges in different cities. I came to visit him. I could see how excited he was to see me. We were together away from our

home-town, away from our friends, just the two
of us. This was a freedom we had not had before.
We had a wonderful time. We went out, had
dinner, went dancing, we talked. It was
delightful and charming. It was effortless. On
that visit I had resolved that I would encourage
Edward into a relationship with me.

But the moment came and went and Edward did
not act upon my signals. He changed the subject.
At the time this surprised me. I was angry with
him. I thought I was mistaken. But on reflection
I knew that not to be true. I knew he loved me.

For reasons even Edward was unable to
understand, he could not let go. He could not
allow himself to read the signs and take the
opportunity, and I did not have the confidence
to press the matter and make whatever effort I
could to understand what made Edward so anxious
and fearful. But I did not and here I am now
thinking of him.

It is said that the most common form of regret
is to do with inaction and that over time regret
relating to inaction can increase in intensity.
I could see the elderly man at the funeral could
not forgive himself; such was the level of his
regret.

I admit that my sense of loss when I now think
of Edward and what might have been has never
dissipated and has, I have come to understand,
become more intense. I know we would have been
happy.

We had our chances. Of course we would not
have known for certain how our life together
would have unfolded but we both would have
seized the opportunity to find out if we had
been emotionally equipped to do so. We were in

control of our fate but equally our own narratives, our confused sense of self and our demons proved to be ruthless, indifferent saboteurs.

I look down at my suitcase. I am going away for a while. I desperately need a break. I have been drifting apart from my husband for some time. Although my marriage exists on paper, in reality it is an apparition. I am going to stay with friends who live in the same city as Edward. I want to contact him but I don't think I will. I'm not sure. Who will I find if I do?

Mr Russell's Essay

In the opening pages of his book *The Problems of Philosophy*, Bertrand Russell reflects on the nature of appearance and reality.

Using the example of the table he constructs an argument through which he raises troubling questions about its existence. His phrase 'the real table, if there is one' will be forever imprinted on my mind.

I really wish I hadn't read that.

As if I didn't have enough to worry about.

I felt my heart beat faster on that morning as I sat, in front of my bowl of cornflakes which stood on the surface of a piece of household furniture the nature of whose existence I was being asked to question.

Inevitably, it never rains but it pours and now I proceeded to consider whether I could in fact taste the cornflakes I assumed I was eating and whether I did sense I was falling because perhaps I had not support from what appeared to be my real seat.

I could of course have chosen to ignore the esteemed Nobel Laureate Mr Russell. Had I done so I would have had to accept that I would be in the minority and a silent minority at that, until now.

Whilst I decided that I had to keep calm, I could not ignore the apparent feeling of tiny beads of perspiration on my forehead and that Mr Russell's postulation did bother me and ruined the rest of my day.

Purchases

I never intended to have a drink on that evening but several hours into it there had developed a neat row of empty bottles of Merlot on the coffee table.

Fortified, it would appear I had made the decision to go online. Acting on a discovery that I was low on toothpaste, within a few minutes, I had selected the 'buy now' option and confirmed my purchase of a 10 pack of Colgate's finest. I was informed it would be delivered by Royal Mail.

This much I do remember. I imagined the knock at the door and a man wearing an ornate peaked cap handing me a parcel as he said 'Your toothpaste delivery, Madam.' Accounting for the rest of the evening is challenging. I can only rely on flashbacks, mostly of the computer keyboard.

I was kept occupied the following week by fielding deliveries. The routine was a knock at the door and as I opened it the view of a man walking away having left a parcel in the porch. By the end of the week, my home and grounds were stacked with items, which included, four metres of electrical cabling, two kittens, a cockatiel, two reclining chairs, two deckchairs, a sedan chair, 25 I litre bottles of lighter fluid, the new encyclopedia of Morris dancing, ten carriage clocks and a life-sized waxwork figure of Orson Welles. On the drive was parked a restored Sopwith Camel Biplane built in 1917 for the Royal Flying Corps according to the owners manual.

I had also received emails which confirmed these purchases as well as a message of thanks for a donation to an Alpaca sanctuary in Peru. With this message was enclosed a photo of the Alpaca I was sponsoring. She was called Maria Jesus Sanchez. Apparently my financial help would attend to her welfare, bringing joy to the life of a formerly lost Alpaca and the chance of a prosperous future.

I had also received confirmation of my enrolment on courses in kayaking, learn Mongolian in six weeks and how to play the harp. I looked over at the instrument I had acquired. It was standing partly unwrapped in the corner of the room, on top of which was perched the cockatiel.

I felt hapless as I surveyed the scene. I also felt dizzy. One of the kittens looked at me and said, 'What the bloody hell are we doing here? You don't like cats!'

I looked at the emails and the photo of Maria the Alpaca. I had always wanted to go South America. I hoped that I would, one day.

Auntie Sylvie's Cat

I had always felt Auntie Sylvie's white cat was judging me and reaching incisive conclusions. This made me feel uncomfortable.

This cat was no usual cat, in many respects. First of all it was stuffed and made of white acrylic hair. It had piercing black eyes and I was loathed to admit, a cute looking nose made of plastic. It was, for eternity, rendered in a sitting position, or perhaps reclining would be more accurate. It was hard to tell. It didn't seem to have legs. It was just a mass of white hair.

When Auntie Sylvie died, the cat had been left to me in her will, along with other objects, including a teapot without a spout, a snow globe from Spain and a complete set of fish knives, along with a stuffed hamster called Gerard.

Whilst I was nonplussed at being left with these items, the fact that I had been lumbered with the cat didn't really come as a surprise. It had been a constant presence in my life long before Auntie Sylvie had left this mortal coil to go off and trouble eternity with her activities.

On my birthday I would receive, as became traditional, a card from her which included birthday greetings from the cat and a photograph of the ball of hair sellotaped to the inside of the card. The cat in its reclining position, immovable and staring. Auntie Sylvie would also end our regular telephone calls by informing me that the cat was well and said hello.

Many of Sylvie's collection of soft toys, seemed, according to her, to have an opinion on all kinds of matters. The disrepair of the local foot-ways, how difficult it was to find a parking space and why the United States should never have invaded Iraq, whilst acknowledging that alternative strategies should have been more thoroughly explored. This was, I had to admit, a view worthy of development from, according to Sylvie, a stuffed Giraffe called Colin.

The white cat didn't seem to have a name. Auntie Sylvie simply referred to 'the cat'. As the years passed, the cat's messages became more elaborate and a few months before Sylvie's death one of the final missives came in the form of a letter.

As the mid 20th century critic and writer Marshall McLuhan once said, 'the medium is the message' and this letter from the cat took my relationship with and understanding of Auntie Sylvie to a whole new level. The letter contained considerable detail on what the cat had thought and done that week, including many visits to the doctors and observations on the inadequacies and successes of the postal service, refuse collection and on the neighbours' comings and goings. The cat seemed to enjoy many Radio and TV shows and had recently discovered 'Netflix' which 'a nice young man' had helped set up.

I could not help but be moved by this letter. All of Sylvie's soft toys and the cat had been her friends and companions, without which, loneliness, not aloneness, would have suffocated her. Sylvie had died. I couldn't dump the cat in the refuse, however much its stare added a sinister air to my front room.

I simply couldn't.

The Pinner Mince Pie Mines

Some of us are aware of the history of the Pinner Chalk Mines which, I think we can all agree, is an interesting and surprising aspect of this part of Greater London.

Few, however, are familiar with the history of the Pinner Mince Pie mines which dates back to the 1820s. This was a developing industry until the last mine closed in 1895 due to imports from overseas including France, whose Tartlet De Noelle, began to take a larger share of the domestic mince pie market.

In addition, the continuing development of methods of making mince pies in the UK contributed to the rapid decline of naturally sourced pies. As a result we will never know the full extent of unexploited fields that lay underground in this part of North West London.

However, using material from Parish Records and on site surveys local Historians have begun to piece together a picture of this 19th Century industry.

Victorian mince pie mining was a dangerous business. The pungent smell of raw mince, sugar and pastry before extraction sent many men insane and to early graves, following long hours underground in claustrophobic conditions.

Post-mortem reports on those who perished also revealed some had died from the effect of eating large quantities of raw pies in a frenzy of unadulterated gluttony.

Following one incident, the refrain, 'Who Ate All The Pies,'twas John Smythe' became common parlance amongst fellow miners. This was the sad story of young John Smythe who consumed so many pies that when attempts were made to bring his dead body to the surface the rope snapped many times, such was the weight upon it. We now know this teasing refrain has been redacted which is another reminder of how those brave mince pie miners have been forgotten.

The process of mining involved men working in two-man teams, one extracting the pies one by one which would then be moved to the base of the nearest shaft by the co-worker and brought to the surface in large heated bins. The busiest times at the pie face were in Summer and Autumn in order to meet the high demand in Winter.

It is believed the shaft of one of the mines is in the area which is now Bridge Street in Pinner and on a site now occupied by Wenzel's the Bakers. When the refurbishment works were taking place grains of sugar and fragments of mince were unearthed. DNA testing confirmed evidence of the human hand on remnants of pastry.

Few clues remain of the mines today, although on occasion evidence of this fascinating past is revealed. For instance, in one case, walkers along Love Lane reported fragments of mince and sugar on the soles of their shoes. These fragments were carbon dated to the mid-Victorian Era.

We as historians and the Pinner History Society look forward to more evidence coming to light of this absorbing aspect of Pinner's past.

Medication

I opened the box and pulled out the metal foil sheets. The tablets were in rows and formed a grid where each pill lay snug in a clear plastic blister pod. Each a brilliant white and each the product of a laboratory and production line.

I took out of the box a sheet of notes which unfolded to reveal text in a small print. I went straight to the section on potential side effects which were listed in bullet points.

'Efficacy and safety' I thought. No medication is 100% secure, but these white pills offered a life, both comfortable and confident, that had been denied me for so long.

Despite already being decided on my intentions I started to read the list out of a feeling that I should proceed on the basis of being fully informed. I read the following;

Potential side effects include:
- nausea, headaches, muscle pain
- vomiting and diarrhoea
- an increase in being more argumentative accompanied by a strongly held belief of always being right
- without hesitation taking offence at being criticised
- an overwhelming need to invade Belgium
- an obsession with the words authoritarianism and elitism

- a sense of entitlement accompanied by a belief in the absolute truths revealed by overthinking

I could live with those, although I didn't like the possibility of the headaches but I was prepared to take the risk. I snapped open a blister and swallowed a pill.

It is now several months later and I can happily report that I am safe and well and feel so much better. I am writing a novel which is very exciting. I sit here at my desk, the sun streaming through the slit narrow arched windows in a neat little prison cell in a little known part of the suburbs of Antwerp.

Nothing

I have been doing nothing. It has been going quite well. I have had to practise. I am quite good now. I think the breakthrough came when I had a transcendental moment whilst staring at the wall for several hours. I didn't see the wall anymore. I didn't see anything, except a sort of microwave background or like the analogue television screen just after a 1970's style shutdown. Nothing except fuzz.

It is tiring doing nothing. Doing nothing is an art and requires discipline. It can be difficult to avoid the temptation of spotting an irregularity of some sort, for example, I noticed an incorrectly positioned knick-knack on the mantelpiece. I needed to move it back to the originally allocated position. I did spend all that time several weeks ago tidying before I started doing nothing so how that object got out of position I really don't know. But doing nothing was supposed to stop me getting upset over such trivialities and to pile on the pressure all I could think about was the economic principle of opportunity cost.

This is not good. That niggling sense of missed opportunity. That assignation that I had so elaborately planned that I did not turn up to in the end, because I was deeply involved in staring at the wall. Or the virtual meetings I missed that my friends were having. My so-called friends. Were they talking about me? I am sure of it. I tried to explain that I needed time. They said they understood. I wasn't sure. And then when they left me alone, I did nothing. It's what I wanted, so why did I feel short changed? They just don't understand. It was their responsibility to examine the value of my original proposition. My so-called friends.

This has to stop! But how do I stop something that is supposed to be nothing. Do something of course. That's better. I will first reposition that object. I have always been fond of that little model of Snoopy the Dog holding an Epee fencing sword and standing in the on-guard position. It was bought for me by that special someone who I left waiting and waiting for me to no avail.

I did fence once, but I hated it.

The Writer

She became drunk at every one of our meetings. At the break she would wander around the room to despatch criticism aimed at anyone who happened to be in range, 'You are not a writer', 'Your poetry is derivative', 'You took that idea from my work', and so on.

One evening she was intoxicated before the meeting had even started. As usual she mingled and issued threats, criticism and occasional praise. When she came to read her work her voice was surprisingly clear, though the front row of the audience had received the unmistakable scent of a cocktail of cigarettes and alcohol. We had a no smoking policy which she ignored. The thought had crossed our minds that if the cigarettes, alcohol and her permed hair came into contact she would have ignited. We put that down to our collective vivid imagination.

Her writing was often an ordeal to listen to and as she began, there was a collective feeling of apprehension although by the end of her set, some had fallen asleep but she did not seem to notice or care.

As the session drew to a close and the last reader returned to their seat and most of the wine had been consumed, she had fallen asleep. Even in sleep she could not keep quiet.

Her head was tilted to one side and her speech was sometimes incomplete and disjointed but we could make out the name Clive which she repeated time and again. Clive was her late husband who had died after a short illness. She was distraught at the time and still appeared to be grieving. Following his death her drinking had increased from its already high level.

In her sleep she seemed to express regret at what she had left unsaid to Clive. She referred to her affair with a woman. This was news to us all. As if speaking with her husband she admitted to her jealousy because of his success as a writer and admitted that extra marital sex of, in her words, 'the most exotic kind', would improve her self-esteem.

In the room we were transfixed and glanced at each other as if to say is anyone writing this down or recording it? We thought she should have written it down. This was the best piece of work she had ever done. Life and Art, Art and Life and a thin gauze between.

No one dared wake her. It was too engrossing, though we were conflicted. We did not like her and yet knew how much she was troubled and merited sympathy. Like an emotional alchemist she seemed to filter her turmoil and convert it into an ability to upset everyone around her.

Eventually she woke and opened her eyes to a room full of people staring at her in silence.

'Piss off,' she said and promptly stood up, gathered her bag and left, picking up a glass of wine on her way out. For the first time we witnessed her vulnerability.

She wasn't at our next meeting and a few weeks later we heard that she had been admitted to hospital and died soon after as a result of the long term cumulative toxic effect of alcohol according to the diagnosis.

We were subdued at the meeting following this news and spent most of the evening talking and in the end decided to honour her by turning the evening into a drinking session.

She would have liked that.

The Burden

As I queued outside the entrance to the British Library I observed the metal frame size gauge and the sign above it advising on the dimensions of baggage permitted to be taken inside. I felt a pang of anxiety as I looked at my bag and back at the advisory frame. I doubted whether it would fit comfortably and I feared it would become irretrievably stuck if I tested its size. I then envisaged I would be discovered trying to sneak in an oversized bag and thrown out by hefty security guards.

In the end I was thrown out but I think that had more to do with the albatross[1] I had also brought with me.

---

[1] Due to the popularity of the poem 'The Rime of the Ancient Mariner' (1797-1798) by Samuel Taylor Coleridge the phrase 'albatross around one's neck' has become an English-language idiom referring to 'a heavy burden of guilt that becomes an obstacle to success'. With this in mind the albatross found its way into 'The Burden'.

The Lifeguard

All Valerie McVal ever wanted to be was a
lifeguard. From the first moment in childhood
when she scooped a sinking plastic duck, a doll
and a bath sponge from the shallow waters of
the paddling pool in the manner of a rescue.

And so she did become a lifeguard, but in her
career of 20 years watching over a stretch of
coastline at Driftwood-on-Sea she had never
been called on to rescue anyone.

There had been false alarms. Many of them.
Such was her zeal and passion for the art of
lifeguarding she had reacted to them all with
a fanatical duty. On one occasion she swam a
mile out toward what she thought was the head
and swimming cap of a bather appearing and
disappearing beneath a choppy sea. It turned
out to be a ball with a swimming cap stretched
over it. Risking her own life in the swirling
waters of a cove she had gone to the rescue of
what was in fact a rubber ring with a shop
window mannequin taped to it. She had never
worked that one out. In another incident she
pulled back to shore an upturned almost
life-size model boat with model figures
representing the crew glued to the deck. This
made her sad because in that replica world they
had all drowned.

Such was her own active imagination, and the
power of the silhouettes which created
illusions on the horizon of the ocean. Valerie

was often presented with these phantoms and
seemingly destined to rescue the detritus from
the sea. It was as if some cruel ruse was being
inflicted upon her. The cruel sea indeed.

Valerie longed to rescue someone. Of course
she didn't wish extreme peril upon anyone, just
enough difficulty that on balance necessitated
a rescue and a dispensing of advice on how to
swim safely in the sea.

On the day when she hauled into shore a
drifting pedalo, Valerie had reached a critical
juncture in her lifeguarding career. This
particular pink and orange plastic paddling
machine had the appearance of a postmodern
Marie Celeste. It contained abandoned clothing
and other personal effects as well as empty
spirit and tablet bottles and a handwritten
note.

This note had been written by Duncan McDunker
a lifeguard on another section of coastline at
Portent, the neighbouring upmarket resort.
Duncan McDunker was a local hero. With the
appearance of a modern day aquatic Adonis, this
played into the fantasies promoted by the press
because his photograph was often in the local
newspaper alongside news of his latest rescue.
Valerie had always been jealous of Duncan.

He was centre stage in moving stories of how
he had rescued numerous cats and dogs and on
one occasion a race horse with the jockey still
caught in the stirrups. This particular inept
stallion had kept straight on when it should
have taken a bend during a race at a nearby
course.

Duncan had saved swimmers of all sizes and
ages who had strayed out of Portent Bay helpless

to resist the strong ocean currents. Most were forever grateful to him for saving their lives although in one incident he had brought a man to the beach who seemed to be drifting and sinking but on reaching safety this man had punched Duncan in the face as he declared that 'he didn't want to be rescued, thank you very much!'

And now Valerie had read the suicide note left in the pedalo. Duncan would never be seen again. The emotional toll of witnessing many hapless individuals terrified for their lives had driven Duncan to his own saltwater grave. Even the gratitude of those left behind had not been enough to have saved this troubled personality.

Valerie was distraught and conflicted but on that day she resolved to leave the coast for good and escape to the countryside and the apparent peace and certainty offered by terra firma.

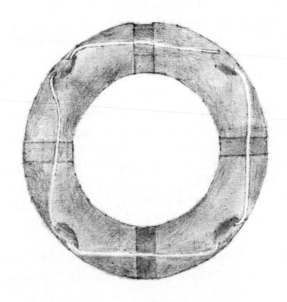

Occurrences at Runway Mansions

Mrs Marjorie Faraday of 23 Runway Mansions was both satisfied and confused. She came downstairs that morning to discover the walls of the kitchen, hallway and reception room, the epicentre of a residents' party on the previous evening, had been repainted in a pastel blue colour. She was sure they were white when she went to bed.

She rang her neighbour and friend, Janet Fitzsimmons who had also attended the party. Janet listened to Marjorie's report and much to Marjorie's surprise did not put it all down to forgetfulness.

In the course of their conversation Janet made her own admission. Recently following a weekend away from home she returned to find her lawn had been cut, her plants watered and new plants planted in a captivating arrangement of colour and shape in her garden. Janet had no gardener unlike many of Runway Mansions residents and so she was as confused as Marjorie and both were relieved to find they had an ally and were not their own.

Indeed they were not on their own as similar conversations were taking place throughout the estate as residents told of experiences where their homes had in one way or another been rearranged, redecorated, refurnished and refurbished in a range of styles without their prior knowledge or instruction.

For example, the lino floor of the front room of Rachel Winkelstein's home had been replaced with a parquet one and the walls of Mary Blight's house had been repapered with a leopard skin pattern. After Mary had recovered from the shock she admitted to her friends she rather liked it and fully adopted that style by procuring a new wardrobe of outfits.

It transpired the key to these occurrences was Number 13 Runway Mansions which was the home of Victoria Frightful, a woman whose presence could only have been described as unfathomable.

Number 13 had been completely reworked in a Gothic style and was adorned with black velvet and leather finishings, a wrought iron staircase and a variety of concealed doors leading to secret passageways.

Victoria, however, was not perturbed and declared this had always been her vision for her home.

She realised, however, that she had to provide a narrative for this epidemic of design activity. To this end she invited the Runway Mansions residents to her home. She told them that Number 13 had previously been occupied by Amanda Architrave, an interior designer, until her death from injuries sustained after falling down an open plan staircase which she was descending from a mezzanine floor.

The inquest into her death, however, reached no conclusion and speculation was rife throughout the estate, fuelled by the news that Amanda's husband had been having an affair with an Architect who had secured the design consultancy contract for the Runway Mansions estate, for which Amanda had also placed a bid.

Her husband's act of betrayal was compounded by his deciding vote on the residents committee for the awarding of the contract.

As a consequence Amanda's torment began after her death.

Victoria explained that Amanda would not rest until she had redesigned and decorated the homes of the Mansions in the manner which reflected each resident's deepest desires and wishes, a skill for which in her earthly life she had demonstrated an aptitude and for which she had not been truly recognised.

The Novel

Scranton Scribbler was writing a novel. This novel was about a man writing a novel. Scranton had been writing the novel for many years and in the novel so had the protagonist, who was called Quinlan Quill.

Scranton had got to know Quinlan quite well as he wrote his novel about a man writing a novel about a man writing a novel. Unfortunately for Scranton he had now found himself cornered in the novel he was writing about a man writing a novel about a man writing a novel and Quinlan had had enough. Quinlan felt he was too well-rounded a character to be left trapped inside a novel about a man writing a novel about a man writing a novel.

When Scranton started writing the novel he was pleased with Quinlan because he was the first character he had written in his novel and so was infused with all the excitement and energy of a wonderful idea.

Of course, Quinlan felt alive too and so one morning when Scranton went to his room for his daily writing session he opened the door to find a man sitting at his desk who fitted the description of the protagonist.

Quinlan looked up and said, 'Who are you and what do you want?'

Scranton supposed he would say that because Quinlan had never met his creator. Quinlan had only ever met the inhabitants of the place where he lived as the man in the novel about a man writing a novel.

Scranton was struggling for something to say and so decided against it for the moment lest he should catastrophically disturb an already fragile situation. He went out of the room and closed the door quickly and surprisingly quietly given the circumstances.

He looked at the pipe he had recently lit and asked himself whether the tobacco was at all unusual or unfamiliar. He decided that it wasn't with little conviction.

He opened the door again. Quinlan was still there sitting at Scranton's desk. Scranton was now annoyed and said, 'Who the bloody hell are you?'

Quinlan looked up and threw Scranton a daggery stare and said, 'I'm Quinlan and I am trying to work and you are trespassing. Close the door on your way out.'

Scranton's resolve collapsed under what had now turned out to be a situation for which he had no reference. He closed the door and went downstairs. He sat at the kitchen table and took a puff on his pipe and a sip of his tea without tasting either although he continued to eye his pipe tobacco with suspicion. The kitchen clock on the wall carried on ticking as it had always done, though Scranton thought it was louder than usual.

He decided to go for a walk as he reasoned with himself by acknowledging that he had been working too hard recently and was not sleeping well. A walk would do him good. He put on his coat and stepped outside.

At the moment of turning the corner onto the

main road, high above him workers from the Plinkety Plonk Piano Repair Company were about to lower a grand piano from a third floor window to take to their workshop. Unfortunately, a bolt on a pulley had come loose and the piano dropped to the ground directly on top of Scranton who was killed instantly.

Scranton lay in a small lake of blood under the fragments of the piano. A crowd had gathered around as the sound of the Ambulance sirens grew louder.

At the writing desk Quinlan had just completed a new section of the novel. He had decided to take it in a different direction from the one about a man writing a novel about a man writing a novel. He had just completed a concluding sentence which read 'as the sound of the Ambulance sirens grew louder.'

He sat back in his chair very pleased with himself and then went downstairs to make a cup of tea.